PARTY IN THE YEAR MMIX

A short novel in twelve chapters

by

John Hartigan Waldo

2009

PARTY IN THE YEAR MMIX

Copyright © 2009 by John Hartigan Waldo

ISBN #978-0-9991756-7-5

Tenth Printing

Cover Artwork: Gary Welter

https://thekaisersbutterfly.wordpress.com/

PARTY IN THE YEAR MMIX

Party In The Year MMIX

by

John Hartigan Waldo

All characters, depicted herein are fictional, resemblance to real persons living or dead is purely coincidental. In particular, references to the City of New Ulm, the work of the Hermannfest Committee, and the ongoing efforts of the Sons of Hermann, and the Monument Fund, should not be construed in any way except admiringly.

CHAPTER ONE

Panic

TEUTOBERGER FOREST BATTLE NEXT WEEK.

BARBARIAN HORDES NEAR; FIFTY MILLION HITS ON CITY WEB SITE TODAY screamed the headlines as the paper hit the tabletop with a smack. The twelve citizens stirred, lifting their elbows from the linoleum, sticky with juice and the sweltering summer afternoon. ONE MILLION VISITORS, SAYS THE SAGE OLD BLOGGER. Distant thunder across the river, another storm before night.

"Look at today's editorial cartoon – shows King Kong dressed as Hermann, standing on the monument swatting at news helicopters."

"I feel like Varus as the barbarians swarmed out of the woods," said Wally, shaking his head. "Here's Amanda's graph on the increase in daily web hits since August 1. Look at the trend also in area campground and meeting hall rentals."

"We may register 21,000 costumed re-enactors by next week!"

"Looks like we'll be 100% booked everywhere, but the graph leads right off your scale", said Gretchen, pushing her chair back in dismay. "You know Munch's 'The Scream'? – that's who I feel like right now."

"Can these projections be true?"

"A million visitors coming here? In one weekend?"

"Hear that thunder? It could be a crowd of our neighbors to run us all out of town."

"Are we past our authority or over budget?" Joyce, sitting between her high school son and a neighbor, answered with care, "We stayed close to budget. And, I met with the Sons and the Council and the festival committee yesterday . . ." Wally interrupted with impatience, "But the invitations, media promises and commitments we made are attracting numbers that could overwhelm New Ulm." Herm thought he'd better head off the panic. "We want a big crowd; the City and the Festival Committee asked us for ideas to attract extra visitors."

A disturbed grunt of throat-clearing or disapproval from the figure in mechanic's coveralls, leaning his greasy elbows on the offending newspaper to avoid his wife's pastel summer frock. "It's out of control – we'll make the city look foolish or we'll expose our town to the chaos of uncontrollable hordes."

"In Rome, they used to throw people off the cliff, for injuring the City."

"When in Rome. . .?"

Dustin and his high school classmates looked white-faced at the confusion and near quarreling of their elders.

"No, when in Mauritius, do as the dodoes do!"

Kurt continued, "Remember in Spring, '69 the word was Zap?" "No," said Wally.

"Zip to Zap. Zap, North Dakota, population fourteen; all the college kids; and this was pre-Internet, just word of mouth and grapevine, descended like locusts; the eat shop and the liquor store were sold to the bare walls by mid-morning. Like one of the new Twitter crowds. A filmmaker from Minneapolis predicts we'll have a mob like Woodstock. The media's starting to circle like vultures."

"Speaking of vultures, eighty-five BASE jumpers are secretly planning a mass jump off Hermann's sword."

"Yeah, we've got four different production companies demanding exclusive documentary rights. They say everybody in the U.S. wants to attend."

"All the pagans in the Western Hemisphere want to watch Wotan's warriors beat Imperial Rome."

"But, Romans were pagans too."

"No, they practiced organized religion. They just collected gods like we collect guns, and for much the same reasons."

"It's bigger than last year's Republican convention in St. Paul!"

White-haired Bert straightened his lanky, octogenarian frame with an almost audible snap. "Herm, you were going to say?" Herm smiled at him and his neighbors, stood up calmly: "We're Okay," he said, drawing out the 'Oh-Kay', "believe me. After the Hermannfest Committee and the Council and the Sons of Hermann organized Hermannfest, we begged to get involved, and they authorized us to supplement their plans in any creative ways we could develop. They'll back us."

He paused for effect.

"You'll not let success spoil your fun? We still have time to call all the people who volunteered to help."

"This is what we wanted all along; to transform a local festival into something regional, something with national, international interest. It'll put us on the map, not just New Ulm, but you and me personally."

Bert contributed: "Folks, everything that's happening results from us all pushing this hard all summer."

"Yeah, like Prometheus pushing the boulder up the hill as punishment!"

"Sisyphus," Marion corrected – "check your Hesiod, by the gods!" with surprising fervor.

"Interesting image though," mused Bert. "Sisyphus rolling the rock upon which chained Prometheus suffers. That'd hurt worse than vultures." Everybody laughed; the gathering relaxed.

"Yes, Dustin?"

"Natural Resources; they'll exhibit bald eagles, and golden eagles at the Monument Park. The Rapture Center, I mean the Raptor Center in St. Paul? A public release of a rehabilitated mature bald eagle. My Dad's still laid off from the plant, so he's meeting tomorrow about Governor Pawlenty standing with the Senior Class to release the bird on Sunday the Twentieth."

"Oh, thank you, Dustin. That's what we need to hear. Good work." Dustin's face lit up more than Marion could remember of late. Megan claimed they'd broken up, but the cell phone records didn't lie.

"The railfans and alumni are chartering a train for a St. Paul to New Ulm excursion that weekend, borrowing rolling stock from the Rail Museum there. It's the annual game between Martin Luther and Gustavus Adolphus. The riders from Northfield's 'Defeat of Jesse James Days' promise to rob the train in front of Twin Cities news cameras."

"Herm, BBC and Al Jazeera both want to set up in Martin Luther College. I thought we'd assigned places through the Police Department.

"Yes, but Al Jazeera won't camp next to Schell's Brewery and BBC has hired Lucy Lawless to drive a chariot three times around the Hermann Monument, dragging a Roman general by the heels."

Wally forced himself to sound cooperative, even conciliatory: "Bert and I have people at the College who can give them rooftop space and set up along with the Twin City broadcasters, those will be representing the national networks. All the local B&Bs are rented out to the Big Bloggers and Net Casters."

"The German, Italian, and Japanese crews will each have a big van, so we mean to park them at the High School, two blocks from the battle."

"The National crew predicts half a million visitors."

Silence for a few seconds, then Wally dropped in with what everyone was thinking: "We're going to need more cops," as visions of mobs of visitors, desperate for food, water, and portable toilets overlaid thoughts of thousands of battle re-enactors losing limbs in an uncontrolled brawling, spilling out of the park base into the homes and down through town toward the river.

"A lot more cops. The Chief says he will get mutual aid from all over the three counties. Same with the Fire Department and the Street Department, for medical, crowd control, clean up. He'll activate the Emergency Preparedness plan at the Mayor's nod."

"At least we don't have to deal with seven documentary film crews." Wally's earlier glumness seemed gone, and the level of excitement of the upcoming festival and re-enactment seemed to drive all humidity and despondency from the room.

"Megan, you've been waiting patiently. . ."

"Oh, yes. Thirty area high schools-sending costumed barbarians. Usually our rivals, but our allies for this event. The

Brown County Fairgrounds are clear for over-flow camps from Flandreau State Park, the KOA people? They'll be open that weekend for sure and the City Parks and the Fire Department plan space for six thousand more campers within the city limits, ok?"

Herm was impressed with the energy and firm voice of the high school girl, he remembered as mouse-like in the first meeting in March. Now she reported confidently to a committee of her classmates, parents and neighbors, who were still stunned by the magnitude of these numbers.

"Wally," appealed Herm. "We can handle it, we can keep ahead, you all feel the excitement, I know you do; all our schemes or wild ideas and solid planning fit into place, like a jigsaw we've almost solved."

"Only the first twenty thousand registered actually get to march in the re-enactment, but with our Auxiliary Viewing sites we can give a battle experience to twenty groups of one hundred tourists every thirty minutes all day long."

"How did we get to this point?" Wally wondered, thinking back.

CHAPTER TWO

The Ides of March

Hermann pointed his sword across the Minnesota River, from the top of his 80 foot pedestal, as a stranger pulled up and parked in the bluff-top park Sunday afternoon in the city of New Ulm. The warm, late winter day inspired many to begin planning events for the time of harvest, still long months beyond this spring's planting. The stranger, hearing talk of the Teutoberg battles walked carefully across the wet grass toward several people, dressed as if they might have just left church, listening to a tall, white-haired man explain Hermann's victory and what it meant to them. The out-of-towner had missed the introductions.

"Kurt."

"Bert, you know Wally Kriendler, and his oldest son Jake."

"Good to meet you again Jake. Good work in the Junior Squad, I hear".

"Herm, let me present my daughter Gretchen Schultz and my granddaughter Amanda, and don't you dears look lovely".

"Oh Pop, we just ducked out of church cleaning early to meet you here."

"Good, here comes my apprentice. . . Michael Cummings, my nephew and media advisor." Herm didn't miss the sidelong glance blonde Amanda gave his nephew.

One last car, a convertible, with lowered top, pulled up, and a girl sprang out, taking her mother's arm as they picked carefully through the mud puddles to the group at the base of the monument.

The stranger responded to a blank look from the woman who dressed and carried herself as a teacher, "I'm just listening to the gentleman's words on the battle; I thought he was guiding a tour."

"He *could* give tours."

The stranger smiled in reassurance, and wandered away down the slope.

"See? We need tours and guides and many of them. This is an opportunity for all of us. We all need to get involved like Herm says to get State and National recognition for New Ulm."

"Humph. That Movie, 'New In Town,' earlier this year was going to do that, wasn't it? And I'll bet SHE hasn't called you, Herm?"

Herm faced Wally. "She's coming back next year to shoot the sequel".

"Never happen, Herm, until we reinstate the film industry tax rebate in Minnesota."

"Oh. Yeah."

"We were the pioneers, with our film board offering a 15% rebate for money and sales tax spent filming in Minnesota. All the states and Canada copied us, then our governor wiped out the program".

"That's right, Clint Eastwood's 'Gran Torino' and the new Dillinger this year? They wanted to shoot in St. Paul and Red Wing until Michigan offered them huge tax incentives."

"I wish Hollywood wouldn't perpetuate that phony "Minneesotah" accent, don'tcha know?" said Marion. "Them Coen Brothers grew up in Minneapolis, and wanted to satirize their neighbors".

"Well, there ya go". Everybody laughed.

"Time to make a movie about Arminius and the Teutoberger Forest; we ran Russell Crowe's "Gladiator" after we closed the shop last night, and I see it's sort of a remake of 1964's 'Fall of the Roman Empire' with Stephen Boyd and Sophia Loren."

Bert said, "I was in a scene with Sophia Loren." The whole group gave instant, respectful silence. "Yes, Miss Loren filmed 'Grumpier Old Men' over in Wabasha a few years back and I was an extra in the waterfront scene." He smiled slightly; so did Herm and Wally and Jerry.

"Kiss custodiet ipsos custodes?"

"Hmm?"

"Who watches The Watchmen?" Michael grinned at Amanda. "You wanna see that movie tonight?"

"'kay." They moved back to the group.

"Why are we doing this, anyway?" asked Wally. "It's just a one-shot weekend deal. Are we going to start trouble?"

"Are we stepping on the Hermannfest committee's toes?"

"No, they want us to test new ideas, trial balloons."

"So, we're flankers, scouts, or exploratii, like the Romans called them."

"Or, guinea pigs, or sacrificial lambs, if things go wrong," finished Wally.

Marion stepped to the center. "I want to encourage young people to study history and languages. Those who don't learn history are condemned to repeat it."

"Or, at least take a summer remedial class", said Herm.

Marion laughed out loud in delight, and gave Herm a smile.

"Seriously, though, I'm promoting foreign language skills for our high-school students to help them earn scholarship money at colleges, plus, volunteering in a big community event will look good when they apply. That was Megan's idea; she wants to organize outreach programs to take Hermannfest to schools and nursing homes; we just came here from visiting my 95 year old grandmother in her nursing home."

Gretchen chimed in: "I know all of us reacted to the announcement of the re-enactment plans as an opportunity to get out of our rut, be part of a big event."

Herm continued, "It feels like we're in on the ground floor of something big, like being in the Yukon Gold Rush of '97. The city council and the Hermannfest committee approve our study group proposing and developing extras for the festival, to fill out the schedule, attract publicity, and serve more visitors." He paused. "I gave them our title, suggested by the German tribe of Arminius: the CHERUSCI: Citizens Helping Event Re-enactors Under-Sub-

Committee (Informal)."

"Pushing it just a little, Herm?" Wally said. "Why not a scary acronym, like SMERSH, or SPECTRE to get us international attention?"

Bert finished for them. "I like the lists you've all made. Areas we can develop to help promote Hermannfest in September. Herm, you and your crew want to develop souvenirs and special tours, Marion, Megan and her classmates' innovative concepts to bring the event into the wider community . . . just brilliant, and practical, if they recruit enough student volunteers. Joyce, you really think you can land some Federal Stimulus Package money?"

"We won't know if we don't apply, paperwork will be ready next week," said Wally. "Meantime, we need more parties, receptions, and food vendors, and I'll get them on paper."

"Cherusci people! Cherusci tri-ibe!

'So proud to live! So proud to . . .'"

"All right, Paul Revere, take your Raiders back to the restaurant. You're closing tonight, Jake," directed Wally, restored to good humor.

Various cars started up. Thumpy music drifted out of two, and the Theme from 'A Summer Place' filled another.

Meanwhile, the stranger scouted through New Ulm, admired the antique homes, elaborate or humble, found the library, museums and bookstores closed for Sunday, almost waved at National Guard women taking a smoke break on the side ramp of the Armory, then looked over the many wide parks and open spaces. Driving past the junction of the Cottonwood River with the Minnesota, he toured the

State Park just waking up for the spring. Along the bottom of the bluffline, he found Schell's Brewery Museum open, and on impulse, signed the guestbook at March 15, 'Exploratio pro Caesar'. He bought a late lunch at Wally's 'Burgermeister' circle tee emm, and drove back to the Twin Cities.

CHAPTER THREE
April

Michael felt little anxiety about addressing a room full of his elders; he and his friends had been invited to present their best ideas, and he knew they had some winners.

Briefly, with the aid of a nearly-antique overhead projector, he outlined the High Schoolers' efforts:

I. "Primus." (he liked Roman numerals)

"Publicity"

II. "Secundus." Visitor Services

(you can make vague ideas seem cut in stone with Roman numerals)

III. Co-ordination with City; and Cleanup

What comes after "Tertius" anyway? Fivesies? Boxcars?

He rattled a new transparent sheet into place:

"One, Publicity," he repeated,

"One event

 Two visitors,

Three participants."

He wondered, 'Image Bank for pre-event Website, where is it?'

He wanted to get to the pictures of his friends.

Here he signaled his friends, who switched on the PowerPoint to fill the screen with brightly-colored images of souvenirs: bronze hairpins, Roman and German jewelry in gold, amber, and precious stones; foam rubber swords for kiddies, plastic laurel wreaths, real laurel wreaths from local florists; yard-sticks printed with local business names and 2-Meter sticks printed the same, to be sold "as swords and spears" for visitors wishing to stand with, but not actually fight the Barbarians or Roman re-enactors. Images and concepts tumbled into the audience of civic leaders and event planners, as from a boundless cornucopia.

Coins, foil-covered chocolate or cornstarch sugar like NECCO and STARK. Cardboard cut-out headbands with tribal chieftain wings, aluminum slugs stamped with the head of Caesar, or Arminius, or Varus, "Collect them all" cajoled Michael, "or trade them for food at the festival, featuring authentic German and Roman snacks from the 21st Century Vendors."

"Pottery oil lamps, first century style. . ." One of the Sons interrupted, "What about the Bobblehead Dolls, young man?"

The Hermann and Thudsnelda Bobblehead Dolls and the Limited Edition "Hermann's Victory" Festival Prints are already sold out, sir, and selling on E-Bay at twice the original price. The Bobblehead of Varus failed because the head kept falling off."

"Just like the original, eh gentlemen," jibed another Son.

As the laughter died down, Michael flashed color still pictures of Dustin, Rafe, and Megan dressed in authentic first century costume greeting Senior Citizens, and reading scrolls to pre-schoolers in the sunlit, open rooms at the New Ulm Library, then signaled for his team to switch on the video.

"Let's go from Outreach to Visitor Services again," and the video showed a dozen people in Hawaiian shirts and straw hats, also young, dressed as "tourists", self-consciously pointing their cameras and umbrellas.

"Welcome folks," said the Roman from the screen, "to the Battlewalk, a brief walk with history that puts you in the Varusschlact, the terrible Battle of Teutoberger Forest. You'll remember how Roman influence grew in Germany during the reign of Emperor Augustus, and the Germans planned to save their homes and families from slavery to Rome." A tow-headed youth in muddy pants and a ridiculous horned helmet, wrapped in a big cloak ambled out of the woods next to the group walking up the narrow nature trail.

"Ah, here's my good friend and trusted ally, Arminius, with news of a rebellion. He visited Rome and studied our military system." Arminius mumbled something and the Roman brightened, "He says he knows you and the Roman Army are invincible in open battle, so we must spread out and hurry to reach the rebels – step lively!"

It looked like Arminius leaned against the Roman, who choked, fell, and shrieked, "It's a trap! Run!" Too late, as a gang of grimy barbarians, shouting and waving spears, leapt from the woods, ran onto the trail, surrounding the tourists.

"And there you are folks," smiled the false Arminius, "three days of running ambushes, driving the Romans like hunted animals, and twenty thousand Roman invaders perished. Sic Semper Tyrannis!"

"Hey, that's not very sensitive in the Bi-Centennial Year of Abraham Lincoln," complained one of the "tourists."

"Well, the school play society has revived 'Our American Cousin' and guarantees no walk-on appearance by John Wilkes Booth," assured Arminius as the video faded amidst laughter and cheers from the Sons of Hermann, and the City Fathers. One councilman muttered to his neighbor, "The next time I have to bring up a sewer bond issue, I want that young man to speak for it."

Prolonged clapping as Michael called his team-mates up to the stage for a group bow. Herm noticed several young women of high school age among them, and reflected that Joyce's idea of sending in the young people to make the first critical presentation to the main Festival Committee would ease all upcoming proposals to that body by the CHERUSCI.

As the assembled membership of the Sons of Hermann chapter and the Festival Committee filed out of the hall, Herm followed Michael, Dustin and their classmates to the side conference room and gave Wally and Joyce a big smile. "What an introduction for our young people."

Wally said, "Yeah, everybody wins. Hermannfest volunteer

work will get young people into the group, and helps them to network with the elders for jobs or college help. Stick around, the students have a new organizational chart for special programs. Some innovative, efficient personnel ideas. My son Jake came up with some of 'em."

Herm sat in back with Wally, as Dustin hauled the folders over to Jake and their squad captain Rafael, who pointed to assignments still vacant and called for help. Great interest in the costumed warrior and chauffeur spots, a lot less in messenger and equerry corps, until Jake suggested people could bring their own motorbikes and four-wheelers, and get gasoline discounts locally.

Food service and school outreach still looked thin so everyone pulled out I-phones, cells, or other electronic amulets, and started texting earnestly to absent friends. Wally whispered to a couple of senior members of the Sons, who'd stepped in behind them, "Let's keep these young people active in New Ulm."

CHAPTER FOUR

May

Herm and Wally strolled into the tavern in State Street, saw most of the CHERUSCI at the back table, and headed to the bar to pick up some Schell's. They couldn't help overhearing a guy almost shouting a conversation into his cell phone: "The Governor's cutting the budget by unallotting? Cutting the State programs will hurt my neighbors! Healthcare, for instance. It's the Legislature's fault – we should go like Nebraska and un-allot our Legislature to a single house. Uni-Cameral, they call it. No not like a Dromedary or a Musk-ox!"

They passed Marion leaning on a booth with a familiar couple; Herm thought the man was Richard from the aggregate company and . . . and Courtney. Marion waved them past, listening to Richard casually lecture, "Sioux Quartzite; the hardest commercial building stone available. Use it in concrete, the pinkish-red stone gives a healthy blush to the sidewalks and streets here in New Ulm. The geological intrusion of Sioux Quartzite runs across the State from Pipestone, through Jeffers and New Ulm, all the way over to Spirit Island."

Richard paused.

"You say the name 'Sioux' now is politically incorrect?"

"Always was. Their own name 'Dakota' refers to the Seven Allied Council Fires."

"Oh."

"I know you moved here to New Ulm, so you might not have a

feel for the history, or History, with a capital "Aytch" as we do. Some of the fiercest fighting during the 1862 Siege of New Ulm was right around where we're sitting now."

"This neighborhood?"

"I'll loan you 'Charles Flandreau and the Defense of New Ulm', Anderson's and Woolworth's 'Through Dakota Eyes' and Corinne Monjeau-Marz' 'The Dakota Internment at Fort Snelling'. And read John Kobles' 'Smoke, Fire and Ashes,' he borrowed stories from the diaries of my great-great grandmother here."

Marion looked around. "I'm writing an op-ed column for our paper here. I want to compare Hermann's war against Rome with our Dakota war here.

"Imagine Hermann on a white horse, just like Chief Mankato on his white horse charging our barricades here in New Ulm. We've thrown out the biased and insensitive phrase, 'Sioux Uprising', remember that?" I want a new name for our 1862 conflict here, instead of the current name 'Dakota War', which sounds like it was all their fault, or happened in Rapid City or Bismarck, or Sioux Falls. I propose 'The Minnesota War'." Herm thought he could see a glow of inspiration in Marion's face, maybe lent to her by the Muse of History.

Wally could see Herm listening, and recognized what he was thinking. "I don't want to touch it. Plenty of families around here, German and Dakota, look at it like it happened yesterday. The Governor signed a proclamation recently reversing the Indian Removal Act of 1863. Let the University, and the State History Bureau take the lead in the Reconciliation."

"Well, we'd better invite, or at least inform the Dakota communities of our event."

"I agree. I know somebody who has good relations with the community at Morton. I'll ask him how we should approach."

Wally's wife Joyce, held a printout list. "Organizations" – Caledonia wants to send their 'Warriors'.

"Historically apt."

"Oxcarts from the Red River Re-enactors coming from Manitoba. They want to be in the parade."

"The Lewis and Clark Expedition's keelboat will be docked at our landing."

"Neat, it's at least 150 years since the last keelboat was here."

"The Sons of Norway will send a High Priest of Woton from the Orthodox Valhalla Church. And there are ten Ancient and Honorable Druids who haven't forgotten the Roman Army wrecking their sacred groves at Anglesey. They will sing curses upon the invaders."

"Some medical historians from Mayo Clinic will be practicing first aid with replica Roman tools for injured re-enactors."

"Umm, better hook 'em up with our paramedics, ok?"

"Anybody else?"

"Walnut Grove's bringing a float for the parade for 'Little House on the Prairie', with Melissa Gilbert riding in a convertible, waving."

"Air Force flyovers? Goodyear blimp?"

"Yeah. Chariot racing from the County Fairs in Northern Minnesota, like Kootchiching County and Rouseau County. They'll race at our own Brown County Fair track."

"Big local sponsors, like Green Giant, with national recognition?"

"A group from Minneapolis, wants to set up a reviewing stand for their people dressed as Roman emperors and senators."

"Good. Maybe we could finally get another Senator for Minnesota."

"Say, here's an avenue . . . pro sports teams, college teams, high school teams, like Caledonia's 'Warriors'. Let's make calls."

"Megan's contacting all high schools and colleges in the five state area."

"Joyce."

"I got the Federal Stimulus Funds approval today – we can do it all."

CHAPTER FIVE
Prom MMIX

Herm drove the long cream-colored Hirondel into the driveway of his sister's house and stomped the Klaxon, releasing an unholy racket. Michael's dependable work in the metal shop, and his preparations for the Hermannfest with girlfriend Amanda, led Herm to offer to chauffeur them to Prom in the antique touring car. "I'm storing this machine for an out-of-towner," said Herm, as Michael slid into the front seat. "He wants it driven for special occasions only."

Then they were in front of her house, and Michael was welcomed inside for several minutes, returning with the radiant Amanda. They were barely aware of Herm or the car, bearing them swiftly to the Prom. Herm pulled in, and honked one short, one long, two short, for "Arminius," as people were lately greeting each other. Several cars answered, one with two long honks, always an insult, but now suggesting "Varus" around New Ulm.

In the crowd at the door, almost all the young women in line reached into their purses – not for mirrors to check their faces – but for Sidekicks, Cells, or a Blackberry to text, or to check their Face (these, of course, have become a new kind of mirror). Long as they don't reach for cigarettes, thought Herm. Time to go meet Wally and the CHERUSCI.

In the entrance hall, Michael and Amanda caught up with Dustin and Megan and the two girls began planning their entrance.

Megan said, "It's so funny. When the girls here quarrel over boyfriends they call each other 'Lupa' and 'Siren' – names they got from the school newspaper, with its list of naughty Latin words. And the taggers and graffiti artists all over town are printing out Latin slogans like 'Romani, Ite Domum' and 'Quis Custodiet Ipsos Custodes?', you know, Romans Go Home, and Who Watches the Watchmen?"

"Oh yeah, I saw that movie."

"I watched it twice."

"Line up guys. It's the Grand Entrance."

The arriving couples stepped through the traditional archway, cleverly painted and distressed to resemble an ivy-covered Roman ruin, but this year with an addition; a computer-controlled sign showing the guests' names in large letters.

Gasps and polite clapping greeted Megan and Dustin, the sign announcing "Empress Livia and Quinctilius Varus." Several camera flashes highlighted the thin beaten gold bands holding artfully piled and coiled dark hair, while 'Livia' swirled through the archway in a layered creation of flowing white silk over heavier floor-length white linen, just concealing white leather sandals.

Next, the sign showed 'Thudsnelda and Hermann' and the room filled with cheers, whistles, and applause as 'Thudsnelda' – Hermann's beloved wife stepped daintily through, clad in a bright, freshly-dyed lemon yellow dress of fine wool pinned at the shoulders with plain, circular bronze brooches, a wreath of woodland flowers in her golden hair. Fifteen seconds of attention, and camera flashes, then time for another couple, but Dustin heard the girls remark that all eyes were on them rather than their dates. Michael heard it too, and they high-fived – delighted that their prudence in wearing plain black tuxes so pleased Megan and Amanda. Neither would have been caught dead at a High School event in a toga, and armor might have offended the school's zero-tolerance weapons policy. So, their only identification now were name tags printed "Hi! I'm Varus," "Hi! I'm Hermann."

The lads led their dates to an assigned table where more flashes made the girls hug each other while Hermann and Varus shook hands.

"Don't look! There's some Goths."

"Well, the black formal works for her."

"Megan, they felt left out, but you convinced them they could defy authority by defying Rome; now Bishop Sarah teaches them the ancient Gothic language at ELC."

"Yeah, they already were into Latin chanting. Some of them signed up for Latin courses at Bishop Jim's invitation.

"He's cool. He was used to people calling him Father Jim at the parish, so now he's Bishop Jim too."

During a slow dance, Dustin had a chance to ask Megan about getting in too deep with promises to the Goth kids.

"Why are they learning dead languages like Latin and Gothic?"

"To perform at Hermannfest; and because by bringing Gothic and Latin back to life, they figure they're speaking an undead language. Very appealing to some of the Goth kids."

"There's another reason, isn't there? Rumor has it you told them the Chancery office at the Cathedral has a copy of a forbidden book, 'Micromoneycon,' available only to Latin scholars."

"Uh-uh. They want the book for certain terrible passages to help conjure up financial con games, wield dark Ponzi schemes; that kind of thing. When the stars are right again, they'll open the portals of risky real estate, and loose the next big series of swindles to wreck the world economy."

"Ohh-kay?" Dustin sounded unsure.

"I just looked mysterious when they mentioned it, and advised them to study Latin to help job prospects and their participation in Hermannfest. Their imagination did the rest."

"Blessed Cthulhu, pray for us!"

"Who's that girl, dancing with Jake? She doesn't go to school here."

"No, she picks him up after practice. Wears a black helmet and leather jacket and takes him to work on her old BMW bike. Name's

Amalasuntha. Artist. Hangs with the Goths. Thought you'd know her."

"Stop looking at her figure!"

"Wasn't."

CHAPTER SIX

Wazustecasa wi (Strawberry Moon)

To make Roman armor Dustin took bars of mild steel flat stock one by one off the rack, sliding them through the ironworker to a measured stop, then methodically clipping them into ten piles of different lengths. For this work, he preferred the whining hydraulic ironworker that crashed its blade through solid steel with a press of a foot on the treadle. Band saws have advantages, but the blades aren't cheap, plus he could punch all the rivet holes with the ironworker. Masses of cottonwood seeds drifted in through the open door and stuck in the grease smeared on the ironworker. Drought stressed the cottonwoods too.

He paused in mid-morning to help the others drag bundles of steel off the semi bed when the delivery truck showed up. It was all he could do to keep up with newcomer Joseph, working the summer in the shop while absent from his Amish community in "Romspreng", as those people designate a Wanderjahr, or walkabout for their youth. Years of farm work gave Joseph quick, sure movements handling bulky objects, reminding Dustin of the valuable physical training in his employment.

When his boss came over with a lightweight angle grinder of green plastic, Dustin switched off the ironworker. "Once you punch all the rivet holes, lightly buff the cut ends with these paper discs to take off the sharp edges. But we're knocking off now for lunch."

Lunch was potato salad and roast beef sandwiches from the 'fridge – and shop talk.

"To bend the armor strips, I think I'll forge heavy bars to shape and weld them to that I-beam scrap to make a jig. Then I can bend all the segments to the right curve using bending forks. Bend them cold, no heating."

"Sounds like a plan."

"But I still don't have a good design for Roman helmets."

"Michael and Joseph and I will finish this big, ornamental gate in two weeks. We'll help you with the helmet and swords then."

"My great-grandfather ran this blacksmith shop with his oldest son until the 1970's, when the farmers stopped bringing in plowshares for repair." He held up a big, crooked piece of curved steel. "See the boltholes where it attaches to the plow, and this point here, I welded it on to replace the worn-off steel. That big washtub-sized canister you're sitting on was the acetylene gas generator for my great-grandfather's early cutting torch; dump a scoop of white carbide powder into the water, clamp the lid tight and the carbide and water make acetylene gas. Never heard the source of oxygen; wish I'd asked."

"Michael, let's grease up the Little Giant."

"I've got to see this."

"Little Giant Power Hammer. Forges metal bars with fifty pound strokes three times a second. Manufactured over here in Mankato a hundred years ago." Herm pointed to the logo on the round drum of the working head held between two pivot arms above the four-foot-tall cast-iron pedestal. Every blacksmith bought one, to beat out plow share points, then the smith didn't need to hire an apprentice or strikers anymore, which led to the decline of blacksmith training.

He thought to himself: 'lighter gauge steel bar than original

Roman armour; I've got to keep the cost down. I can make a buck or two. The dealership is sponsoring twelve sets for the football team, so they can march with the visiting Roman Legions.'

"Keep those points greased up," as Michael applied the grease gun, "and maybe we won't have to replace the Babbitt metal bearings this year.

When Michael turned on the blower and ignited the big trough-like gas forge, which roared into life, Dustin pulled on plastic goggles and a heavy air filter mask to protect eyes and lungs against dust from grinding. He remembered Herm pointing to a brand new computer that had broken down from the shop dust, and the implications of similar trouble with breathing and vision exposed to thick grinding chips and particulates.

Dustin wouldn't risk his I-Pod in the shop, and the protective ear plugs cut him off from others while he cleaned up the last segment of Roman armor. Should be enough for twenty sets; his friends would meet for a big session of assembly; he'd assured them their football pads were hardly lighter than Roman armor – that had done the trick. Why didn't Megan return his calls? He thought they'd had a good time at the Prom. He set the last curved segments into numbered shipping boxes and wondered if Mr. Wendzell would spring for materials for another twenty-five sets of lorica segmentata and helmets. If not, it looked like the basketball and baseball teams were all signing up for German costumes. Dustin thought about the Army recruiter, but didn't want to act this year, before he saw college scholarship numbers. He liked metal fabricating – maybe the Navy needed machinist's mates.

He saw Mr. Wendzell wave at him from the main door; looked like his Dad's pickup out there. Michael still desperately held a long iron bar as the Little Giant beat madly on the other end that glowed yellow-hot. Joseph tended more bars heating up in the gas forge and watched to learn Michael's forging technique.

"Your Dad's here, Dustin. I'm not working this weekend. A wedding and two graduation parties. Read through this manual by Monday, then we'll juice up the EDM."

"Electrical . . . ?"

"Discharge Milling. The Soviets invented it, I think. With practice you can use this little hot wire to cut out round bar die blanks in hard steel to stamp out those doubloons and souvenir coins you want to make for the Festival. Monday. Early."

"Hi, Dad."

"We gotta get home and figure out the Digital Conversion Box for your Grandmother. She says the last time people had no television, it was the nineteen-thirties Great Depression.

CHAPTER SEVEN

Divine Julius

"'Hermannfest – A Monumentous Occasion,' from one of my classmates," said Megan.

"Another bumper sticker; besides going on the web site."

"Have you seen some of our bumper stickers around town?" asked Marion. "Honk for Hermann. Then simply, 'dit dah dit dit' for Arminius, 'Three Honks for Thudsnelda' and what else, oh, 'honk if you love Venus', 'Honk if you are Venus,' 'I brake for Cherusci,' 'My other car is pulled by goats.' All printed here in town at the shop I work at. I'm sorry we printed those thousands of 3-inch-square 'Hermann Wants You' stickers, with the Winged Helmet Chieftain-character pointing at the viewer; they're showing up on all the wrong places."

"Theodore and his friends sent along a whole packet of pen-and-ink cartoons, some of which should go on the web site, like this one, depicting the Hermann statue holding a large spoon above the caption 'The Walker Loaned a Famous Sculpture to New Ulm' as Amanda held up a large illustration board. Here's a series of clever cartoons, signed "Gotha" with a feminist symbol instead of an 'O'; see, the Roman and Germanic goddesses of love, both struggle over a heart silhouette.

"And this one, Donner and Jupiter throwing lightning bolts, like darts, at a target. Nice pen work."

"Here are full-color paintings of the characters heavily influenced by Howard Pyle and Frank Frazetta; extremely muscled swordsmen in dramatic poses. Say, did Hermann ever have to fight giant snakes, or swarms of bat-men? Is this Thudsnelda, riding a sabre-tooth tiger? Maybe we should sponsor a competition for art and heroic illustration."

"Put it all on the Internet, the artists can donate part of their sale price to the Monument Fund the Sons of Hermann set up for improvement," suggested Wally.

"Look at this design," exclaimed Herm. "Can you silk-screen this on a T-Shirt?"

"More good news; the Students at the College got their play accepted at the Minneapolis Fringe Festival at the end of the month."

"That awful Roman revival?"

"Yup. Plautus, with a lot of his original digs at religion, plus ribald jokes and slapstick."

"Speaking of slapstick, please show us what your friends have produced on video, Michael?"

The screen lit up to show a bright red Smart Car pull off the road, and about a dozen fur-clad barbarians tumble out, their movements speeded up by the camera, accompanied by frantic player-piano music. They each produced several spears and threw them at a large target, turning it into a pin cushion.

"Hey, I know where they filmed that," said Jake. "It's an archery range the other side of Mankato."

No dialogue, just that wild piano. Suddenly the barbarians looked off-camera, made extreme double-takes and excessive gestures of surprise as armored Romans advanced in a line. The barbarians threw up their hands, ran around in circles bumping into each other, scrambled into their car.

Cut to a highway scene as a pick-up truck with Roman soldiers standing in the back, waving their swords, chased the little car up the road, as the screen faded to:

"Hermannfest September 18, 19, 20 New Ulm"

and the web site address.

Next, a gloating Roman officer twirled his big curling mustache and sneered at the camera while his armored minions seized a struggling girl and chained her to railroad tracks.

The scene cut to noble Hermann galloping on his white horse.

Cut to a speeding train.

Close-up of struggling girl's face.

A close-up of Hermann.

The TRAIN.

HERMANN, fade to

Hermannfest September 18, 19, 20 New Ulm.

Amanda spoke up, "The next one is Megan's and my idea." Across a flowing brook Lady Roma and the Spirit of Germania waved spears and scowled at each other; then threw off their classical robes, under which they wore high boots and lady wrestler outfits, and leapt savagely to meet in mid-stream, splashing, as the screen showed "Hermannfest September 18, 19, 20 New Ulm."

"Megan!"

"Mom, you can't even tell it's us."

"Listen, Michael. How about straight-forward fight scenes?"

"We're shooting a single – combat this afternoon. Theodore and his friends from Ess Seeyay are teaching classes in First Century combat to our high school re-enactors."

. . .

". . .upload to hard drive by putting a CD or jump drive in the console. Oh, hi, Theodore, we're almost set up."

Theodore the Goth, age seventeen, unbuckled his collar of black leather and chrome studs, replacing it with a plain steel neck guard over his padded jacket, while a taller opponent already helmeted stepped up beside him. He addressed the assembled football and baseball teams.

"My loyalty is pledged to this Canton of Nordly, covering southern Minnesota, so to help you to prepare as Roman and Germanic fighters, I'll spar with the winner of fights all over the Midwest, Magnara from Mankato."

Theodore slipped his steel helm down, saluted with round shield and padded practice sword and started trading feints, then heavy strikes with all his weight.

Few swings, mostly jabs, like a boxer or knife-fighter.

Over in seconds, he shouted "Good," lowered his shield and sword, stood still while the victor stepped back.

Both fighters saluted again, burst into a flurry of clattering, thudding blows, while the team started to shout approval. Even with careful footwork, Theodore was defeated in half-a-minute, stepped back, dropped battered shield and sword, and pulled off his helm.

Cheers went up as Magnara from Mankato slipped off her

casque, dramatically shaking out brilliant red hair.

"Theodore and I will demonstrate basic moves with you for First Century combat, and we invite you to the upcoming warrior tournament in Wisconsin to see really powerful fighters."

Rafe caught up with Theodore after the sparring sessions. "That looks as rough as Golden Gloves. Who are you people?" Theodore didn't mind a compliment from a Varsity athlete.

"Ess Seeyay: Society for Creative Anachronism. Megan Rhodes recruited us for Hermannfest. We hope to field a single-combat against somebody from Gemina Martia Vitrix Legion."

In the college theater, Amanda helped Michael record three players dressed in wild wigs and short tunics dancing in front of a Roman merchant and a soldier. The soldier points a small metal amulet at one of the dancing servants -- they all stop and one reads slowly from an ancient scroll of the "Aeneid." The soldier impatiently points his amulet again, and the servants go into an act predating the founding of the city.

Formio: We can't get anything good since they decimated the entertainment.

Grumio: Don't you mean 'digitalized'? Nyuuhk-Nyuuhk-Nyuuhk (smirking)

Stichus: I'll digitalize you (sticks 2 stiffened fingers in Grumio's eyes)

Grumio: Ow-Ow-Ow-Ow-Ow. Woof! (makes ancient gesture).

Formio: Looks more like binary to me, heh, heh.

Stichus: Oh, a sooth-sayer, eh? (pokes with fingers)

Formio: Ow-Ow-Ow-Ow.

The high school girls' sewing club looked over the pile of fabric and leather for Hermannfest costumes, then called in their mothers, aunts, and grandmothers. The mothers recognized the opportunities to get their children to show up at church, and organized sewing bees at churches. The daughters summoned their friends with texting and instant messaging for heavy fabric cutting. Turned out, the boys were glad to get experienced advice and help on historical costuming for their First-Cinch warrior outfits.

As they set up tripods and packs at Amanda's church, Michael said "We'll replace anything that doesn't receive enough hits on the web site."

"So we need footage of everything related to Hermannfest," finished Amanda. "Those guys in Sleepy Eye with the rap about Hermann? Can we trade more airtime for a limited permission?"

The guest speaker had laid out numerous fabrics, finished clothing, and books on tables in the church basement auditorium, and looked personally too polite and outgoing for the First Century barbarian clothes he stood up in. "My wife and I have created theatrical costumes, party clothes, and historic weave, hand-stitched where it will show. I'll show you today cost-cutting and time-saving tricks for an honest representation of First Century Germanic garb. We often portray Viking-age people around the Midwest and we're making Fourth Century Danish clothes for a Shakespearian troupe's Hamlet in original era costumes."

"Your First Century German wears tunic, trousers, shoes, maybe a hat, maybe a jacket or a cloak. Slide one here. The tunic hangs straight down, with no flare-out – unlike Medieval tunics. Big, rectangular, stubby sleeves."

"Sounds like a Norwegian craftsman's shirt."

"Yes, ma'am, a lot like that, but no collar and no cuffs. You belt it in."

More slides. Jackets, trousers. Slides of dresses.

"Women's dresses. A tube of wool. Pin it together at the shoulders and let the rest drop, front and back. The upper part hangs over the pins, so we can get away with blanket pins from the fabric store. Here's a slide of one woman's dress made with a little hood from the back flap."

"Wool, preferably twilled, woven wool – no felted wool – that's from the eleventh century."

"Subdued colors – a green from mixing blue and yellow. A medium dark-blue. Lemon-yellow from dyeing with onion skin – so it's not colorfast."

"Photo here of original two thousand year old dress from Huldre Bog nearby in Denmark, about the end of the first century Bee See."

"Sketches of Germanic Tribesmen and Tribeswomen from Max Barsis' "The Common Man Through The Centuries" with some good, working class Roman costumes. Some good colors here in Osprey's 'Rome's Enemies'."

"All these are on the CD and handouts; the sources and the bibliography in the back of your packets of patterns and materials."

"Excerpts from Margaret Hall's monograph on Ancient European shoes. Shoes will be either a flat piece you step on, pull up and draw together, tied shut at the top, like I'm wearing here; or I've got a pattern to cut out of one piece of leather, the open-work sandal kind of thing."

"Like the Roman's caligae?"

"More of an upper-class fancy shoe; maybe right for Hermann and Thudsnelda. Like this pair we made for Megan Rhodes' prom outfit," and then the costumer held up a tangle of brown, leather straps.

"I'll stick around the rest of the afternoon to help you get started."

"Remember, unless you encounter Stitch Nazis or hard-core re-enactors who count stitches per inch and look for mistakes, no one will hoot 'FARB!' at you or scream 'ANACHRONISM! RELEASE THE RABID BABOONS!'"

Giggles and guffaws faded and Hilda Cummings said, "I'd rather you didn't use the Church's new Singer for this heavy fabric, but the children's costumes are light enough for it."

. . .

Canoeing down the Cottonwood River in the late afternoon, under perfect summer skies, Marion thought she'd share a few stories. "I've worked part-time three years now at the Print Shop; oh, and isn't it funny, we're starting to see Hermannfest bumper stickers all over town. My favorite is 'My other car is drawn by cats'. We'll have to have everything ready soon. Once school opens and the harvests begin, none of us will have extra time."

The Cottonwood River gurgled along to keep the conversation moving, and Herm twisted his paddle to avoid a sandbar.

"I sold grain dryers for nine or ten years until, remember, we hit dollar eighty corn. Then that big terminal fire two counties over and all the liabilities. Everything else came apart too. . . Bert gave me space behind his feed store to set up the auto repair shop, then he helped me get a loan to reopen Grandpa's fabrication shop next to my house.

I think we can bring a certain level of manufacturing and industry coming back to New Ulm and the Minnesota Valley, and I intend to help some worthy people get into it. That's part of why I jumped into the effort for Hermannfest."

Marion nodded, "I want more opportunities here for our children. Too many don't have enough money for advanced education. Special events like this raise historical awareness and our place in history.

Half the population of all Brown County lives in New Ulm, and we're losing numbers."

Herm nodded.

"I support the wind farms proposed for our Bluff Line near town. If we generate power, that could bring manufacturing back. Employ our kids, y'know."

A terrible scream from some big raptor bird patrolling the river up ahead. "If that's an eagle, I'd call that a favorable omen," joked Herm. Marion looked sharply at him, "I thought you had no religious beliefs."

"Hey, 1 dropped out of the church, but I'd say I'm more agnostic, more doubting and skeptical, than closed-minded."

He thought for a moment. "See, I watched the movie 'The Vikings' – ya'know, with Kirk, and Tony, and Janet, and Ernest the night before the big, third grade catechism test. All I could think of was that great rowing tour up the fjords, the fighting, pillaging, laughing uproariously; and the Viking's Code? So, the principal asked me in class to recite the answer to question #37 'What is a happy death?' I stood up – and – instead of something about a state of grace, I said 'To die with a sword in your hand, atop a heap of your foes.'"

"Testifying for Odin, huh? Your sister tells it different."

Herm suggested, "Let's close the curtain on that clash of the faiths."

In the evening, they strolled over to join the neighborhood families cheering their children's softball game.

CHAPTER EIGHT

The Advance of Augustus

"So we've finished Bavarian Blast for this year 2009; I'd like to check their attendance to see if the publicity for Hermannfest carries over to the other events," Gretchen suggested as she checked traffic in the rear-view mirror.

Marion mused "City of Festivals, we call New Ulm. The Romans filled their calendar; during the summer's driest month, on 23 July, they would celebrate Neptunalia, to pray for rain, by setting up shades they call umbrae."

"Now we go to the lake and put up beach umbrellas," said Joyce, as the car pulled up in front of the church's meeting hall.

"Thanks again for helping my Grandma get out today. It cheered her so much to be by the water again."

"Marion, our families remember how much she's done to get new people settled in our town. She's always been the first to greet newcomers," Gretchen assured her.

. . .

"We meet three times a week now and we're on the phone all the time."

"That's good! The Hermannfest Committee and the Council are giving us more responsibility to follow up our ideas."

"Or more rope," suggested Wally.

"Listen, we're getting heavy interest from the networks. The Midwest correspondent -- you know Cynthia – has been here twice to scout, and she won't discuss actual national plans for coverage, which we think is a favorable sign," opined Bert. "A production company from Chicago is applying for city permits this afternoon, according to my source at City Hall, and it sounds like others want to film here. The City Attorney's looking over release forms for local icons like the Hermann monument."

"German and British TV reps have talked to the Festival Committee, "said Joyce.

"Good."

"Are the attendance numbers for New Ulm festivals restricted or proprietory?" asked Joyce. "I want to see if our efforts are helping Bavarian Blast or RiverFest or the County Fair." The committee passed around some charts on paper.

"You heard that goofy song 'Hermann the German' on the radio all week? A novelty tune like 'Alley Oop' or 'Ahab the Arab'. Shows we're getting into national conscientiousness."

"Any notice from the late night comedians?"

"They're still trying to recover ad revenues torpedoed by the digitalization."

"Is that what you think it was about? Remember those noisy tests of the Emergency Broadcasting System? This was the final test, shutting down broadcast TV."

"Hold on. The paper say 94 percent of Minnesotans say their digital conversion is O.K."

"Huh! 98 percent of Americans would never admit they can't get their television to work right. All that freezing, lost signals."

"Conan O'Brien. He promised to broadcast from the Minnesota State Fair. Should we invite him; no, Conan the Barbarian Schwarzenegger, he could swing a movie sword like he uses to cut spending in the California Assembly. Gretchen, write in those names."

"Here's the new opera, 'Hermann und Thudsnelda' premiering in Chicago in November, by Gunther Schuler?"

"More cartoons – Hermann arm-wrestling the Green Giant. Emperor Augustus wandering the streets of New Ulm, looking for 'his lost legions.' Suggestion that Schell's Brewery – already offering Hermannfest Beer – add '9 A.D. Root Beer'. Log all these; and the television stations are running series of old sword and sandal movies to compete with HBO's 'Rome,' 'Quo Vadis,' 'Ben Hur' 'Son of Hercules versus Mothra' . . ."

"Can we restrict helicopter flights within a certain distance of the battle? We don't want it to sound like First Air Cav is coming to support the First Century Warriors."

Wally introduced the new topic. "The Hermannfest Committee is calling for our best ideas on the public Teutoberger Battle, to compare with their own concepts. We all want a thrilling spectacle but nobody needs to see the actual butcher's work of Roman Legionnaires and German tribesmen really hacking each other to pieces."

"But aren't these experienced re-enactors?" asked Marion.

"The Romans we invited from Milwaukee and Chicago are experienced, and know the dangers of their weapons, but some of our visitors are dressing as German barbarians for the first time and have little training with sharp, heavy weapons that can stab people, or crush Roman helmets," responded Herm. "Michael brought some props here." He gestured as the young man held up a thick, painted plywood shield pierced by two vicious spears, then a crested steel helmet almost sheared in two by the hatchet head still jammed in it.

The Committee and Cherusci members present didn't make much noise.

"We've been talking carefully with military re-enactors with decades, even lifetimes of experience."

"Problem with battle re-enactments is when two hostile forces collide, like at Gettysburg."

"Our civil war re-enactor friends tell dreadful stories about the early Civil War Centennial battles in the nineteen fifties and early sixties when Civil War buffs pulled great-grandpa's musket off the wall 'to see if it still works.' Sure enough, way too many 'Johnny Rebs' and 'Billy Yanks' stuck each other with long, sharp triangular steel bayonets before folks figured out, 'Yup. Still works.'

Many casualties, also from 'blank' volleys of gun fire between opposing ranks at close range. Guys forgot to remove the long steel ramrod with which they'd just stuffed a charge down the barrel. Muskets were fired with no bullets, but a very lethal steel ramrod came whistling out of some of them, to the discomfort of their opponents out ahead. Nowadays, ramrods are collected at most Civil War and Revolutionary War events, and nobody faces off anymore. Units may demonstrate tactics and maneuvers separately, and fire volleys away from crowds, at target range. Look at the Civil War movies – the actors all have soft rubber bayonets."

The appalled silence deepened as Theodore the Goth stepped up in thick, padded armor.

"Spears, arrows, and rocks still kill people, as our friends in pre-gunpowder battle play tell us."

"They say, 'don't perform live steel clashes without extensive practice and choreography, like stuntmen or trained stage fencers.' Even padded weapons require long experience, with all parties following the same combat rules, just to avoid serious injury.

"Melees, or wide-open, free-for-all fights are too hectic and confused for untrained fighters. Think about those big face-crushing shields the Romans carry. Don't want my face bashed by three layers of willow covered by hides and bronze fittings. Without a face grill, you'll get your nose busted – not to mention eye injuries when even blunted spears start flying."

Theodore held up a compact disc. "Here are SCA rules for combat; minimum protective gear styles."

Bert thanked the young Goth fighter, and addressed the group, "We can get away with avoiding a direct confrontation of armies because Varuschlacht, or Teutoberger Forest, was a running battle and slaughter, rather than a collision."

"We're recommending in writing to the Hermannfest Committee, to reinforce and support their plan the following battle rules:

1. No face-off or scrimmage between Romans and Germans. When the Germans move menacingly toward the Roman lines, do not engage. The Romans must fall back in feigned confusion before the Germans advance closer to drive them toward the barrier wall. Again, Germans and Romans must not collide.

2. All spears must remain held vertically – Romans and Germans alike. Spears are defined as anything you're holding in your hand. Do not lower spears horizontally; do not throw spears.

Nothing may be thrown, except during separate demonstrations on target ranges. Any bare swords must be held vertically from beginning of re-enactment. Do not draw swords or knives; do not drop your spear or shield. Stay in your group, unless you are a designated 'Hero.' 'Heroes' must not actually engage opponents.

3. Spears and swords may be rattled (swashed) against shields loudly, and war cries and slogans may be shouted. (Please, only classical allusions – avoid modern vulgarities or personal slurs.)

4. Standards, banners, trumpets, drums encouraged.

5. No war dogs, chariots, elephants, venomous creatures, cattle stampedes or other animals permitted, except for mounted characters like Hermann and Varus, and then only behind the lines, when armies get close.

6. No scorpions, onagers, ballistae, firepots, or palisades, spikes or other siegeworks, except that clever German barrier wall, to be identified and marked beforehand.

7. Sherriff's deputies and police officers will monitor re-enactors' weapons handling. Videotaping will be used."

"Whew. Will that do it?"

"We'll have uniformed police to reinforce the rules, and for crowd control," confirmed Wally.

"The Hermannfest Committee is drawing maps for street department and police to mark off visitor areas and viewing sites, separated from Battle areas."

"Oh, and Number Eight: All captured or surrendered Romans to be given drinks and good wishes and safe conduct – and not sacrificed to any forest gods, ok?"

"Business to the Council: do we want a temporary ordinance or a variance for lawn signs promoting Hermannfest? Check on it with City Hall."

"Police working with City workers and Boy Scouts to distribute flyers door-to-door, advising people to lock their doors and monitor their neighborhood during the Hermannfest Weekend, because of the large number of visitors."

"Make sure every municipal employee, local or visiting, who works during the event gets a complete souvenir package – many will miss attending with their families."

"Here's the first official spear carried in the 2000th Anniversary Reenactment, made here in town of locally milled Minnesota Valley hardwoods – 2 meters long. No, we won't be throwing these either."

"How about our documentary maker, the guy from Minneapolis? He wants a couple of his friends running around with cameras in our re-enactment battle?"

"I don't know. Do they permit battlefield reporting in Civil War events?"

"No, but let's give the networks several clear locations all around."

"Back to attendance numbers; the Festival Commitee hasn't issued numbers of attendees, but it might be comparable to Bavarian Blast – you know, twenty, thirty thousand max."

"Guys, we may have that many costumed re-enactors."

"You're kidding!"

"You know my friends in the First Minnesota, the Civil War re-enactors? They went to the reenactment of the battle of Antietem, bloodiest day in American history. Thirty thousand civil war buffs."

"No."

"In their twelve hundred dollar kits with rifles."

"How much to outfit a German re-enactor next month?"

"Thirty, Forty bucks if you make it yourself. And plenty of people will show up with just rudimentary outfits as German barbarians; you know, horned helmets, bearskins, a rake handle and a garbage can lid for a shield."

"A million people in Minnesota claim German ancestry. More than that in Wisconsin. Our festival has caught fire in their imaginations."

"Where do we draw the line?"

"We must not exclude anybody who wants to express cultural heritage."

"We can rank the best costumes front and center and flanks."

"I agree. We'll need impromptu judging and clan assignments. Hand out these three page souvenir brochures to everybody, which explain joining the German tribes to resist Rome – Cherusci, Chatti, Marsi, Bructeri. Tribal chieftains, animal totems, plant or foliage badges, dress codes, war cries, and – most important – rules for re-enactors. Oh, and include a membership application for the Sons of Hermann and their monument fund."

"Media consultant predicts that if we line up five thousand tribesmen, we'll make the nationwide evening news, Saturday."

"Huh."

"Fifty thousand spectators and counting."

"With five weeks to go, where will these numbers go?"

"More fundraising gimmicks. Auction off positions as tribal leaders to benefit building fund; raffle off German barbarian outfit; costume contests, combined churches sponsoring open-to-public costume ball; separate admission fee."

"Bishop Jim reminds us this is the Jubilee 'Year of St. Paul' commemorating the two thousandth anniversary of the birth of the apostle."

"Yup, put it on the site."

"Heavy interest in the internet from people identified as interested in Renaissance Fairs, Ethnic Dance, and European Travel. Let's use these numbers."

"So, you're projecting for a hundred thousand people?"

"How many till we reach Woodstock proportions?"

CHAPTER NINE

Donner's Day

Hobnailed boots trampled woodland flowers as the Roman Legionaires marched into the clearing. Sunlight glinting off their armor alerted a sturdy German youth, leaning on his painted shield beneath the trees. Without even drawing back into the shadows, he shifted his spear to his left hand, set cow horn to his lips and blasted out three long bawling calls. He fixed his glare on the startled Legionnaire, pulled out his cell phone, and texted his friends with details. His girlfriend roared up on her BMW motorcycle. All this was followed by several television camera crews, broadcasting live in Minnesota and Germany. One camera crew followed the couple as they drove around town, bearing the news, then stopped at an elementary school. Early plans had Jake rent a horse and ride through the town, shouting "The Romans are Coming! The Romans are Coming!"; but he'd talked the CHERUSCI out of it, convincing them the time was better spent addressing more grade school history classes.

The camera crew stored Jake's shield and arms in their trunk, so he wouldn't disturb zero-weapons policies, and followed Jake and Amalasuntha to the gymnasium, where the principal led the assembled history students in the growling cheer of greeting. Ten minutes of pointing at ready maps, teacher's hands shaken, and bags of souvenir coins handed to them, and they departed for three more appearances. Later, the teachers planned to march their classes a couple blocks over to get history lessons directly from the Romans.

The camera crew already had footage of Michael and Amanda

speaking at a nursing home solarium, and also Megan and Dustin appearing at a church council luncheon; enough material for 30 seconds at 6 and 10 (or, 1 pound, 2 and 6 pence, as the BBC crew still joked).

Twenty-five of Michael's classmates worked as a volunteer team with the City crew, placing trash cans, barriers, setting up benches, shades, and the rest station, and working to clear undergrowth and trash, and improve sight

lines in the public viewing areas. A good opportunity to remove prickly ash, European buckthorn, and other intrusive plants that choked marching and viewing areas. Also, check for lurking poison ivy patches.

Visitors from out-of-town thronged to the Roman encampment on the high ground while campus security from Martin Luther College coordinated with Brown County Sheriffs' Deputies, and City police to control parking, give directions to tourists, and set up road blocks. Television crews followed preparations, interviewed rowdy college partiers, and compared costumes of arriving re-enactment groups. The TV people had learned to follow the people with the heaviest shields, longest spears, and thickest clothing, as likely to win the upcoming costume contests. The Chinese television crew was delighted to learn, while interviewing Jake and Amalasuntha, that her old German BMW bike was built under license in China. The Chinese commentator borrowed Jake's cloak and shield to ride with Amalasuntha past his cameras several times. "Next, Drusilla and I will cook Chinese dishes fit for emperors", mugged Amalasuntha, pushing her goggles into her hair.

Dozens of small camps were set up on the bluff-top around Hermann's statue, at the level parkland along the base of the bluff, and everywhere in between. Hermannfest committee members, and their helpers recruited by the CHERUSCI bustled about with clipboards, blackberries, and walkie-talkies, greeting the arriving re-enactor groups, checking them in, sometimes in squads or companies, sometimes in regimental numbers, guiding them to camp sites and motel accommodations.

Herm, Michael, Amanda and their neighbors and classmates assisted judgment calls from Hermannfest referees on costume authenticity, assignments to the ancient fighting tribes, and identify likely trouble makers.

Megan said, "Dustin and I anticipated the problems of college-age youth looking for a wild party. See what our friends from Mankato have done to our family celebration of Fasching in February."

"They took over with their binge drinking, fouling every tree, and lots of this" (here Dustin made a motion as though flipping up his shirt).

"So that's why you designated a Markomankato tribal affiliation for everyone who just wants to get drunk, and won't march with Hermann? Brilliant!" said Herm.

"Yes," affirmed Megan, "remember, the Markomanni tribe in first century Germany wouldn't join Hermann's fight, even after he sent them a very graphic 'heads up', and they later actually opposed him."

"So, auxiliary battle walk site number 6 in the southwest ravine will sell lots of beer and see some of our volunteers dressed as Roman and German warriors, pretending they're the central battle. Also, lots of uniformed police and paramedics moving around to maintain public order. We'll divert everybody over there who just wants to partayhearty, without spoiling the main show," finished Dustin.

"We'll be doing all this again tomorrow and Saturday too, to keep everybody sorted, so we're arranging assisted shifts of our own people to help Hermannfest officials and police."

Still two days until the Teutoberger battle re-enactment, and the level ground was filling with tourists, re-enactors, and CHERUSCI volunteers roaring around on their four-wheelers and scooters carrying out errands. The rest of Thursday, Dustin, Michael and other volunteers sold chances at the Sons of Hermann booth – three javelins for a dollar, to stick it to a large painted Roman target. All proceeds going to the Monument Society fund. Membership brochures were freely distributed, along with schedules of the weekend's events. Their classmates from public, Lutheran, or Catholic high school, spent considerable time on the Roman camps trying out their Latin language skills with the Legionnaires visiting from Milwaukee and Chicago. They traded hot pizza for first century Roman rations, but under Minnesota's new host/liability laws and the watchful eye of the Centurion, together with

local law enforcement, they couldn't talk the troops into providing the under 21 crowd with Roman sour wine rations.

With homecoming the weekend following Hermannfest, many of Jake's friends got permission during this civics educational project to miss classes, but missing football practice was unthinkable, making coordination of schedules an exercise in inspired winging it.

Just before sundown, word came that Sheriff Rich had released an official estimate of ninety-five thousand visitors parked or camping around New Ulm, up seventy-five thousand from Wednesday. Extra police, fire and emergency personnel were alerted from all municipalities of the nearby five counties. Projections for Friday and Saturday showed three hundred thousand visitors heading for the re-enactment. The mayor also called nearby school districts to assist with buses and drivers for public access to the event.

"It's like watching floodwaters come up in the valley," remarked Wally. "Some visitors from the Red River at Fargo and Moorhead say their lakes and aquifers are full in a long, wet cycle while we're in a severe drought this year."

CHAPTER TEN

Freyyha's Day

Leaving the grand banquet after rubbing shoulders with invited dignitaries in the Turner Hall, Herm escorted Marion to the MMIXer gala charity costume ball sponsored by the combined churches as a joint fundraiser. Rumors on television and the internet suggested it would be the party of the year, with celebrities, film stars, big politicians making the scene. Certainly, a school of predatory-looking leather-clad paparazzi snapped to attention, then relaxed, as Herm and Marion strolled up, held their first century pottery lamp/exclusive/passes to all events and entered. "Today was crazier than yesterday," Herm said. "The sheriff estimates a quarter million visitors this weekend," asserted Marion. Walking into the broad, lofty hall was like walking against a heavy current, the sound was so loud; that, plus the press of bodies. Excited voices completely drowned out a band in the back. "So many historical costumes, I really feel underdressed."

"I like it, let me get you a drink." He stepped into the excited crowd and it felt like stepping into the surf. Not a decibel below roaring, but still a happy, anticipatory mood.

"Let the Games begin!" said the man dressed as Caesar.	"All that electrical work?"	"Yes, he said, it's just a rumor."
"Expect a decision any day."	". . . he's appealing."	Not as appealing as he thinks, thought another.
"Won't disc it until Spring."	". . . sixteen gains. . ."	"shortens a player's career."
"Played for the Vikings." (laughing)	". . .drink?" "Please."	"I don't think they can. . ."
". . .a State budget shortfall."	"Can't hurt the economy."	". . .harvest forecasts good across the U.S."

"See Caractucus and Vercingetorix? Won't talk to Varus and Augustus."

"See the Empress?" "Yeah, the dude? Same as Cleopatra over there."

They look sharp, though, whoo!"

"What about loans for next year?"	". . .so instead the Russians and Chinese intelligence will monitor and expose our crooked financiers."
"Why would they help us like that?"	"It's Chinese money we're squandering."
"Imagine! Them protecting Wall Street from itself."	"Well, the SEC won't."
". . .Neo-Crime?"	"Same old crime we let them get away with."
"Hyper-inflation?"	

About here, by the bar, Herm slowed down to eavesdrop.

"Two please." "Not all the benefits are good."

So much laughter in the hall and constant ringtones announced banquet guests who kept jumping up to take their calls outside for better reception.

"Darling, listen to my music."	"Battery's dead. . ."	"That dress she's almost wearing?"
"As the bishop said to the actress. . ."	"Who's she with?"	
	"Got my email?"	"She's got eligibility for one more year."
"Wild amusement and laughter. . ."		

"My other car is pulled by goats," laughed the burly, red-bearded man, dressed in a fur tunic and rough leather boots. Herm thought, "well, he's ready for the battle tomorrow."

"enough diplomatic people to hold the G8 right here."	"This is the time."	"That was well done."
"I'll drive him back to Minneapolis Sunday afternoon, following the parade."	"He uses people like video game characters."	". . .closed at 98 today."

"Herm, with the battle re-enactment tomorrow, this event is like the dress ball right before Waterloo," and Marion nodded to brightly-clad people milling about.

"Senator Franken's hosting Saturday Night Live is what I've heard."	". . .general tax revenue."	"Saturday in Hong Kong."
"...dressed as Freyyha?"	"see the bodyguards, some rap star – see his posse and their bling?"	"Arnold?"
		"Lucy and Spielberg?"
"There with the German consul and the governor of North Dakota, see?"	"Emperor Augustus and the Federal Reserve Bank in Minneapolis."	"More paparazzi flashing. . ."
		"Over there with Angelina, Reese, and Jennifer."

A long-haired blonde, who looked like a television news anchor, seized his arm, smiling with insistence. "I just know you're a Leo," she gushed. "Because I'm a Libra!"

"I'm Ophiucus" declared Herm. "The Thirteenth Sign."

"But there isn't. . ."

"I got my sign legally changed."

While she was still giggling, he carefully stepped away with the drinks. "What's all the cheering?" People crowded toward the doors. "Let's go."

"Look, the actors playing Hermann and his wife Thudsnelda just walked in with the mayor."

"Bet you could hear the applause in Sleepy Eye."

"Look at her eyes," a resident said with awe. "She's not from around here, as they say."

"Wow, she's. . ." "Better go talk to her," said the tall farmer, who might have been anybody's uncle.

The national guard recruit needed no more urging, neatly leaped forward, holding out his hand. "Here is the last rose of summer. For you."

"Liebchen!" said the brunette to the recruit. Herm watched some of the flirtations.

Herm handed most of the glass, with such liquid as hadn't sloshed out to Marion.

"Your health," he said as more talk, gossip, and clatter tumbled around their ears.

"Don't put your money in that again," a bright, young man said with a nod and a smile. "Keep your money in town, believe me." "Those kids will benefit from the right words," advised a tall, neatly-dressed, glamorous lady, whose name tag read, "Hi, I'm Venus."

Marion nudged Herm and said "could be."

"Belgian government looks for fifty thousand European re-enactors for bi-centennial of Waterloo in 2015. People I know are preparing their gear!"

"The kids are worried about the Mayan calendar coming to an end in 2012, and the world with it," said Marion.

"Fear not, the next five years are about re-birth, and honest talk," a Scandinavian matron assured her with a pat on the shoulder in passing.

Marion stared into the crowd. "Who was that?"

Herm said slowly, "I've been watching the interactions. It's funny who won't talk to whom. There! The high priest of Woton, ignoring the Druids." "I'll introduce you." "Thank you." "Liebchen!"

". . .well, they're pretty stable."	. . . they own a house together."	". . . get the appropriation through the legislature."
". . . the mayor's address?" "I don't see them." "is it Kate or Renee?"	"...wrote a serious paper comparing pre-Christian religions of Germany and Romans . . . synthesis, plus Roman Central Authority, . . . formed the church in Europe."	". . . point spread for Sunday's game?" ". . . Missouri Synod offer him a job?"
". . . the right words!" "didn't think they ever left Manhattan" "Emperor Augustus and the Secretary. . ."	"call me" "two guys dressed as Laurel and Hardy." ". . .everybody else is here tonight."	"not this one, or the next, but the idea is sound." "Call them Monday." She's shaking hands with all the local women."

Herm watched the grey-bearded Priest of Woton stare at the brightly-clad newcomers who'd established themselves in the northwest corner, staring in obvious awe as a lean, one-handed warrior quietly conversed with the National Guard people in their camo battle dress. "Norm!" "The . . . Chinese consul." "I'm sure that's Elizabeth" "behind Jennifer and Jessica?" "George, baby!" The public address boomed: "ALL VISITING DEITIES, PLEASE SHOW PROOF OF DIVINITY TO RECEIVE FREE NECTAR AND AMBROSIA AT THE BAR" "I thought there was magic in the air!" "We should pick up the young people, get them home before 1:00, like we promised." "Xena!" "Xena!" "Xena!"

"That's the lady who rode as Epona, the mare Goddess of the Gauls and Romans," Herm nodded to a tall equestrienne who smiled as she passed.

"She looks it," Marion said, some disapproval and warning tinged her voice, he thought.

"What? She's a veterinarian south of town. Don't see any Valkyries tonight."

"Just as well."

The party noise and movement resembled random Brownian motion observed a science-minded observer from the musician's gallery above the north end of the hall.

An hour later, the party peaked just below critical mass. Still, all that energy and tension had to overflow. Couples drifted toward the exits; more urgent affairs to be explored.

. . .

"More Fireworks?"

"Heat lightning. Must be 50 or 60 miles away."

Sheets of lightning flashed, outlining the flanks of white thunderhead palaces. All silent – too far away for thunder.

"Oh." Spears and jabs of jagged branched lightning, twisting light creepers, filled the horizon, ripping along from east to west, like sizzling powder trains burning across the clouds.

Swords, whips, lances flashed back and forth behind the towering walk of thunderhead castles. Volleys of light answered instantly from the other horizon.

"Looks like a battle."

"As between Imperial Rome, marching to enslave the world, and free people."

"An eternal struggle between privilege and human rights, concentrated power, and personal liberty."

Cloud-armies outlined her words.

"This is why I teach history. The American Revolution isn't over, and history isn't old things, but our current experience, happening again."

The cloud-warriors traded lightning bolts back and forth between bullwarks of mountains, shields of quivering light.

"Hermann and Thudsnelda and their people didn't just win one battle. Like Hercules, they struggled all their lives."

"Look at that! Those flashes, half-hidden, but stretching all across the sky. That's how I feel about you."

Another rippling light display showed no more speech was needed tonight.

Along the horizon, the hero-horde clashed with all the Legions of Rome, spears of lightning flashing behind the ranks of clouds. The cloud-giants continued their war, Donner strode with lightning across the land. The people found their beds, considered the next day's battle, thought of their children, fathers and mothers, ancestors, slumbered, dreamed of harmony between past and future, success and promise. It seemed they laughed with old friends and others they hope to meet. Fathers and mothers reassured them, maybe a shining young boy waved, someone remembered Freyyha singing her blessing upon the herds and the little ones. The rich Valley slept to the murmur of the River and the little River. Clouds of peace and contentment drifted. . .

Then, an hour before sun-up, it rained all over the place.

CHAPTER ELEVEN

Battle

It quit raining for the early morning, outdoor Yoga class, and the clouds cleared off before the 10 a.m. Fun Run.

"Dowble-U, Eye, Inn, Eee Radio broadcasting from Hermann Heights above beautiful downtown New Ulm," blared the loudspeakers mounted on the mobile station van.

Several thousand German tribesmen encircled the Roman encampment, supplying their understanding of history to visitors swarming through the camps. The roar of the crowd was constant, but the content shifted, as one moved around. On the East side, vociferous tour guides from historic sites all over the country formed the Chatti tribe, or 'Chatty" as they liked to say, and chanted Latin phrases to harangue the Romans. One heard phrases like "Da vinum' (Bring wine!), 'Bibe' (Drink!), 'Reple' (Fill up!), and 'Romani, ite domum' (Romans go home!) picked from 'Sons of Hercules' movies and 'Monty Python."

On the West, the Bructeri, mostly medical students or college fraternities, held contests to deliver impromptu harangues at the Romans: "Yeah, Romans, think you're so smart! Haven't even switched your calendars to A.D. yet! Yeah!" "Our thunder god's bigger than your thunder god!"

Those tribes on the North included multitudes from Burning Man and Rainbow Fest, with brightly dressed pagans, witches, Renaissance Festies and Infesters, wizards, and radical fairies, and Live Action Role Players, all dancing and waving their arms as several white-garbed Ancient and Honorable Druids plucked their iron-stringed harps and intoned dreadful curses against Rome, the Emperor, the Legions and their bodies and weapons. Other tribes in the shadow of Hermann's monumental statue simply chanted 'Hermann! Hermann! Hermann!'

John and Marty and their other friend John, dressed as First Century German tribesmen in dull yellow tunics over rough trousers and brown, plastic flip-flop sandals, complimented the imposing kit of scarlet tunics, polished armor, and weapons of the two Romans guarding the gates of the chain-link hockey and soccer fields, within which the visiting Roman re-enactors had established their tents and equipment stands.

The visiting Germans saluted the exquisitely-armored Roman Tribune, who lounged indolently on a padded couch, shaded from the bright, morning sun.

"Excellency, may we worship at your personal altar, there," asked John, nodding respectfully toward the bronze figures of Mars and Fortuna displayed on a small table. Rome's Finest Son indifferently regarded the barbarians through eyes that expressed superiority, and he casually stated, "Oh, you're not worthy," turning his attention to his perfect manicure.

John and Marty smiled and said, "thank you, Sir, thank you," backing away. They caught up with their other buddy from the Twin Cities, John, dressed as his Romanian tribal ancestor might have, with blue paint stripes across his face, that just shouted 'Death To Rome!' They watched armored Romans wind up a box-like ballistae of well-joined timber, then loose a three-foot bolt at a high angle down range to a distant target zone, clear of people. "Oo, wouldn't want to be in front of that," opined Marty.

The day went slow for two Roman soldiers standing guard at the main gate of their camp, nodding to visitors, drifting in and out.

As the soldiers looked past the Brown County Sheriff's Department car, toward the tribes, one said "Hey, Marcus?"

"Yeah, Julius."

"Did you see what became of those anti-fur demonstrators?"

"Looked like they were jostled considerably when they tried to spray-paint that Chief's bear skin loin cloth."

"Yeah, but those nice New Ulm police rescued them. That one police-woman winked at me. I think she likes me."

"Marcus."

"Yes, Julius."

"Why are those British, Gaelic, and Germanic women all flashing us.?"

"It's a traditional insult or curse among Northern tribes. I like the one on the right. I think she smiled at me."

"Marcus, hear that? The tribes are singing new words to a 'Sixties tune:

"Please Mr. Varus, I don't want to go!

Forward ho-o!

There's a German tribesman with a spear, fixin' to poke me in . . ."

"Be quiet. The Centurion's watching us!"

"Marcus."

"Yes, Julius."

"Who's the idiot playing 'Garry Owen'?"

"What?"

"You know. . . General Custer's theme song. There. In the German camp. He's playing a wooden fife."

"Well, the cross-pfeife is a German instrument, but Sixteenth Century, rather than First Century Germany."

"Here's the words, circa 1715:"

'We'll break the windows and bust the doors,

We'll knock the bailiffs to the floors,

We fight and shout till we get hoarse,

So join us in the chorus!'

'Instead of spa, we'll drink brown ale,

and we'll pay the reckoning on the nail,

No man of ours,' – here his voice almost cracked on the high note,

'will go to jail, for Garry Owen and glory!'"

"Yow! Custer went out but didn't come back, just like Varus and the Legions were massacred."

"Seems to me that the Roman invasion into Tribal Germany resembled European advances into tribal America, you know, trade, settlement, some military clashes."

"Yeah, some parallels there. That's why we dress up for re-enactments – to study and teach history."

By noon the Centurion figured it was time for his own Psych Ops, so he marched four unarmed Legionnaires toward the gate, while the German tribesmen shouted and jostled with anticipation.

Linking arms, the Legionnaires recited:

'The poor, benighted German,

He thinks to follow Hermann,

He'll die like any vermin,

The poor benighted German!'

They performed the Rockettes' high kick, pivoted together and marched away.

The mob of tribesmen and tribeswomen looked confused, and offered no clever rebuttal, so everyone applauded with faint clapping and dispersed.

"Marcus?"

"Julius."

"Why didn't we bring our Gatling Gun, I mean – our ballistae and scorpions?"

"Because the Burghers of New Ulm don't want six foot long spears or balls of burning pitch rattling across Minnesota Street again."

"Marcus."

"Yes, Julius."

"Will Mitra accept us into heaven if we do our duty as soldiers?"

"No Julius. Worship of Mitra isn't established in the Early First Century. We'll probably spend eternity in Tartarus or some German Ratskeller."

"Hey look, the Centurion's discussing battle plans with the German chiefs and the Hermannfest people."

Marion, Gretchen, and Joyce stole a moment from their duties to meet and watch preparations for the Teutoberger Battle Re-enactment.

"You know, the people of Pipestone closed down their long-running 'Song of Hiawatha' pageant. We may want to repeat this event."

"But there's only one two-thousandth anniversary."

"How about an ongoing project of Hermann's later battles, and the tragic parting from Thudsnelda? The cycle could run for years. Chariot races at the county fairgrounds, automobile demolition derbies staged like gladiator games, history plays here in town."

"And a parade and food vendors? Let's work on it."

They all recognized the possibilities.

"We'll start drawing up proposals after church tomorrow."

From a balcony on the Hermann monument, Amanda checked in with the CHERUSCI organizers.

"Make up three big signs, and make regular PA announcements as follows: 'No firearms permitted in the re-enactment performance area.'"

Everyone called her at once.

"Amanda, what's going on?"

Herm's voice was clearest on the walkie-talkies.

"Michael saw a Chatti tribesman with a big old Mauser broomhandle pistol stuck in his sword belt. He alerted the tribal chief, who's ordered all such weapons handed to him for the duration."

"You copy that, Sheriff?"

"Affirmative, deputies checking assembled tribe leaders now."

Further radio and cell traffic confirmed busy and careful searching.

The time for the scheduled battle approached, and Bishop Sarah excused herself from the opening convocation, suggesting that less ecumenically-minded members of her flock might not favor her praying with pagans, real or mock. Prayers to Tyr, Hercules, and Saint Cuthbert went up anyway.

Dustin reported in: "Those clever Goth kids! They convinced the priest of Wotan that our sham battle, instead of a real one, meant that his promise to sacrifice a goat could be fulfilled symbolically. So, Rafe's brother brought up a Pinata for him to burn. We better keep an eye on those druids, too."

"Yeah, no 'Wicker Man' re-enactments please."

At the opening of the pageant, the chiefs and the holy men of the German tribes, and the Roman consul as head of his country's religion, blessed their followers and called on their antique deities for good luck. Several thunder claps raised cheers among the Romans, looking to their right and shouting "Jupiter! Jupiter!" until the Germans pointed out the New Ulm Battery firing salutes from their field pieces. "The thunder favors Germania! Success to Hermann and the tribes!" they shouted. Cheering roared up through the watching crowd.

A tipsy Roman made a big show of approaching the Natural Resources booth where a huge, adult Bald Eagle looked around and glared, while perched on display to promote wildlife education.

The tipsy Roman, "The priests want to read that chicken's entrails for a good omen." The DNR officer politely waved him away. Someone else noted the tethered eagle from a great distance, and soared swiftly over the crowd to get a good look and to emphasize his territory. Everybody assumed that the approach of the bald eagle so near them indicated a favorable omen for their side.

More excitement swept the field as a thin domestic ginger cat chased a late-appearing thirteen-striped ground squirrel across the open space, the television cameras of the world following the desperate scramble of the little beast. As the cat inevitably closed in for the kill, a quick-thinking girl sprinted out shrieking, startled the cat, allowing the rodent to gain a nearly-concealed burrow, and escape. Boo-s and mumbles of discontent for the interrupted sport were overwhelmed by rising cheers as people remembered it was their own state symbol just saved from destruction. The cat sat down and made a careful show of washing her paw.

As one German warrior said to the other: "Don't listen to that Roman fortune-teller, the augur. I only use an auger in January, when we go ice-fishing!" Cheers, and much toasting of Hermann with carelessly-quaffed beer.

In German camps, spectators and non-combatants gradually shuffled into designated viewing areas. Some last minute arrivals of re-enactors demanded assignments.

"Cool, look Michael, the Rumanians showed up dressed as Dacians. They're carrying long, curved war hooks."

"They can march with the Marsi tribe."

"The Italian Consul from Minneapolis – full regalia as Roman Consul, with six Praetorian guards marching with the Chicago Roman Legion."

"Uh-oh, the Minnesota Star Trek Fan Club in full costumes."

"I'll handle this, Dustin," said Herm. "Romulans and Vulcans: please march on the flanks as Roman Auxiliaries. Klingons," to a trio of tall, bearded warriors dressed well enough to appear in movies or the next TV series, "you'll fight where you want, of course, but please don't wave those two-handed batleH around? Star Fleet: observers status only, ok?"

Herm looked at another gaggle of medieval costumes with lots of wild hair and pointy ears, who crowded up to join the fun. Some with green or blue-painted skin too.

"Hobbits, orcs, magic trolls, elves, kobolds, will you help the German tribes establish the Slaughter Wall lines against that chain link fence, please?" "Uncle Herm, it's Darth Vader and the Storm Troopers!"

"Aw, that's too much . . ."

"No, it's the band for tonight's street dance."

"Oh good. Rafe, you copy?"

". . . ive by five boss, we'll take 'em to the stage."

Then it was five o'clock and the lengthening shadows helped bring antique darkness to the Minnesota woods.

John told us later, "as trumpets and war-drums sounded to assemble the warriors, we found our German tribe in a circle cleared of visitors, on the flat fields between the wooded bluff and the chain link fences of the soccer field."

The multitude of visitors, holding up cameras, cell phones, and small children (some of whom waved cell phones) almost filled the open, flat ground.

The re-enactors realized that the mass of people had formed a new Forest, through which the Romans could march, amid cheers, to join battle.

"'John, still wearing your sunglasses?'

"'Prescription; I don't want to miss anything.'"

Varus led his column of Legionnaires, while the Chatti, the Marsi, and the Bructeri tribes crept through the shadows up ahead.

Wearing a tall helmet with large, golden wings Hermann (in his secret identity as Arminius) waved goodbye to Varus, and swung his people, the Cherusci scouts, away from the Roman Army.

As soon as the Cherusci vanished into the woods, a scout brought news to Varus, shouting loudly that Arminius was wounded and his troops surrounded. War drums sounded from behind the trees. Varus ordered his troops toward the darkening woods.

Little boys, watching from the chain-link fence by the battlefield below, cried out "No, no, don't go in the woods!"

A horrible clatter poured out of the trees where Romans and Tribesmen could dimly be seen struggling. War cries and howls of triumph reached a crescendo as Romans struggled out of the terrible forest, followed closely by shouting warriors shaking shields and spears and flags, and sounding horns. No overlay of music from the finale of '1812 Overture,' although measured drumbeats from the woods would have benefited from the ominous Latin chanting in 'Carmina Burana.' Uniformed deputies and police officers cautioned the excited viewers to set down all beer cups, cameras, pets, and small children, lest they be tempted to throw them at the remnants of the Roman Army staggering past toward a narrow pass held by more Germans.

"I knew better than to fence with the tough-looking Legionnaire facing me, so I just grinned at him, shook my spear-shaft up and down so he could see I wouldn't whack him. He moved in, faked a gouge at my gut, and I yelled, dropping to the ground. Twitching, I mumbled 'good job, mate!' as he moved down the line. A couple more ticks and I jumped up, ready for another fight.

"I found another of the Roman re-enactors from Milwaukee, and like the originals, he didn't waste breath on battle cries, but watched me hold my shield aside, encouraging him to take a stab. So I took two deaths at Teutoberger Forest!

"Praise Wotan! That Milwaukee Centurian told me later that the only problem they had from us German re-enactors was the nine-year-old boy who would run up and kick their shins."

Another charge of shrieking savages drove the panicked Romans into a narrow corridor, under constant attack by swarms of angry tribesmen. Less a battle, than a riot, as wild men rushed forward in vengeful fury against their oppressors, carrying all before them.

The Romans tried to make a stand with their bugler cut down in mid-tune. Blood thirsty cheers from the German barricades and the public areas as General Varus shouts something, raises his sword desperately, and falls behind the last standing Romans, who are cut down by advancing tribesmen or hustled away in chains.

Some expensive-looking battle standards are waved jubilantly by Germans who hold them before the new triumphant Hermann, universally cheered by the roaring mass of spectators as he strikes a familiar pose beneath the huge, metal sculpture on the bluff, and raises his sword over the heads of his people in protection and blessing.

As a conquering general, Hermann would receive a triumph the next day, a holiday parade through the City, with his troops, chieftains, captives, loot, and some neat old cars too. Maybe an antique fire engine.

But tonight, a man and a woman, both bishops in their churches, accompanied the aged figure of the Pipebearer as he sought out the German consul, who called over the Mayor, who beckoned to several young people born in the Minnesota Valley. A little smoke went up, pictures failed to be taken, and later, the reporters and newsmen questioning all those present never did hear what talk was made.

CHAPTER TWELVE

Triumph

Heard along the parade route on State Street:

"Hermann!" "Hermann!"

"Hermann!" "Old Roman custom for a slave to ride with the triumphant general, whispering memento mori – 'remember you're mortal'."

"Snow cones! Hot dogs!"

"The banner says they're the Cherusci tribe."

"Look at their funny shoes."

"Mommy, I'm scared of the hairy men!"

"Oh, they're just wearing furs."

"What about that one? He has claws, and they're leading him on a chain. Whoo!"

"The Chatti tribe." "What're they singing?"

"...that old time religion,

it's good enough for me!

Let us thank the God of Thunder,

To fail would be a blunder,

He helped us get some plunder,

He's good enough for me!"

"The Marsi tribe. They've got a Roman officer in chains."

"The Bructeri. Hi, guys!" They waved back, and threw some doubloons, or drachmas, instantly scooped up by the little kids.

"Oh my God, Dustin! When we get married you can take my last name and be Dusty Rhodes!"

"Well, maybe when I break into country music." "Cue the dobroe and the bass."

"Nice Mercedes."

"Look at that Studebaker."

"The Forty-nine, or the wagon pulled by four grays?"

"The dachshund's wearing a chain mail shirt and a Pickelhoub!" "I like those fuzzy, white Spitz dogs." "I don't think those little dog breeds were around in the First Century, but they're sure cute."

"Who 's the old dude riding with Wendzell? And what kind of car is that?"

"It's the only Hirondel in the world, and he's the original owner. Patricia doesn't like flying, so he usually comes to America by himself."

"Those smokey little cars can't be anything but the East German Trabant two-cycle."

"Like smoke? Look at this Opel truck. It's running on wood chips."

"Yeah?"

"I read about it. That big water heater thing is the 'holzvergaser," generating fuel by destructive distillation of wood chips. Commonly used in World War Two Europe."

"Steam tractor, look! Whoo! Whoo!"

"There's one! I told you there'd be old fire engines!"

"Getcher pickled bear meat on a stick! Good for German warriors."

"Plastic helmets! Plastic swords! Show yer support for Hermann!"

"The New Ulm Marching Band! Go Eagles!"

"Tim! Jackie!"

"Getcher genoowine plastic head of Varus! In a genoowine plastic Roman helmet! Surprise your friends!"

"Is that Renee in the convertible?"

"Renee! Renee! We love you!"

"Who are all those characters riding by?"

"People from Minneapolis dressed as First Century celebrities."

"Is Cleopatra a dude?"

"Looks sharp though."

"Who brought that half-track? That's a German one-ton D-11?"

"A whole pack of BMW cycles? Nice."

"A flock of Valkyries, riding Vespas. Sweet."

"Stay back! Stay back! Don't taunt the Romans!"

"Wow, they look tough."

"The Re-enactment Legio Vee Eye-Eye-Eye-Eye-Gemina Martia Vitrix from Chicago and Milwaukee. Good form."

"Salve Romanes. Civis romanis Sum."

"Sky, earth, road, stone, steel cuts to bone. Sky, earth, road, stone, steel cuts to bone."

"A thousand paces, two steps each, ya know, to a mile."

"What about a kilometer?" "Who cares?"

"The nursing home people are throwing rose petals; the Romans are saluting them. That's cute!"

"Roman workmen following the Army, blacksmith, butcher, carpenter. Do you see the little boy walking with the carpenter's tools? Do you see him Smiling at everybody?"

"Is he. . .?"

"Why not? He said he'd come back."

"No, Mike's a carpenter in Mankato, and that's his son Liam."

"The Saint Paul Mayor's Pipe Band. They've stopped to play in front of the reviewing stand. They're introducing a new tune written by the Pipe Major for Major Tony Clunn, the discoverer of the Battle site. It says here 'the opening doubling on C represents the double-tone of his metal detector.'"

"They're marching off to the tune of 'Tenth Battalion Highland Light Infantry Crossing the Rhine.' Hope the German Consul can take a joke."

"Jaunty tune though."

"Everybody's dancing."

"Father, those are the Mennonites from Manitoba of whom I wrote you. They report success logging with those oxen."

"Yes, please introduce us after the parade."

"Look at that! Look at that! Look at that!"

"The new CD1 Dornier flying boat. Beautiful."

"Pilot in Spirit Lake logged a flight plan, with approval to fly over the parade route."

"Well, I think that's everything."

"And here come all our fire trucks. Parade's over."

"No, what's that shooting? Galloping horses!"

"It's the James Boys and the Younger Gang. Robbed the bank in Northfield! And Xena's chasing them in her chariot."

"And a motorcycle and sidecar with Cherusci tribesmen chasing them all!"

Then the people of New Ulm, their children, and their guests, wandered away to find food and rest, and reflect on the gifts and sacrifices of their ancestors.

PARTY IN THE YEAR MMIX

End

NOTES

PEOPLE THIS STORY IS ABOUT:

I. The CHERUSCI Committee

Bert - Farmer and feed store operator in New Ulm

Gretchen Schultz - Bert's daughter, supports the church

Amanda Schultz - Gretchen's daughter

Kurt Schultz - Father of Amanda

Wally Kriendler - Restaurateur and businessman in New Ulm

Joyce Kriendler - Accountant, the brains of the outfit

Jake Kriendler – Son of above

Marion Rhodes - Teacher, mother, worries about the children

Megan Rhodes - Sees some possibilities

Dustin – High Schooler

Hermann Wendzell - "I think I can make this work."

Michael Cummings - Hermann's nephew

Amalasuntha – Goth girl on motorcycle

Joseph – Amish farm boy

John, Marty, and John – Re-enactor dudes from the Twin Cities

Marcus, Julius; The Centurian; The Tribune – Look more like Romans than the originals

II. Parties of the Teutoberger Battle

- Arminius, alias Hermann the German, heroic leader of First Century, A.D. Germanic resistance to Roman invaders
- Thudsnelda, beloved wife of Arminius, "Thud" for short
- Publius Quinctilius Varus, alias "Varus", Governor of Germany, Friend of Caesar
- The Cherusci, the Chatti, the Marsi, the Chauci, the Bructeri, the Sicambri – Hermann's Fightin' Tribes
- The Marcomanni Tribe – Prefer Romans and didn't fight
- The 17th, 18th, and 19th Legions – 20,000+ doomed Romans

III. Other German Heroes

Martin Luther, Arthur Schopenhauer, Frederick the Great, Catherine the Great, Johann Sebastian Bach, Count Zeppelin, Otto Lilienthal, Claude Dornier, Richard Wagner, Rudolph Diesel, Hildegarde von Bingen, Ludwig von Beethoven, Til Eulenspiegl, Marlene Dietrich, Friedrich Nietzsche, Immanuel Kant, George Frederick Handel – wrote opera about Hermann and Thudsnelda

IV. Pantheons

- Donner – red-bearded Lord of Lightning, Thunder, Rain
- Freyyha – goddess of Love
- Tyr – god of righteous, manly struggle
- Wotan – god of magic and knowledge
- Julius – one-twelfth of the calendar
- Augustus – get the Senators' votes and become Immortal in your own lifetime!
- Neptune – god of the waters
- Pluto – god of wealth
- Jupiter – god of storms
- Saturn – darn good car
- Mars – god of manly virtue
- Mercury – god of merchants and communications
- Morpheus – god of dreams
- Vulcan – god of smiths
- Venus – goddess of Love
- Cupid – god of Love
- Cthulhu – god of Lovecraft
- ChacMal – god of rain
- Chango – god of thunder
- St. Cuthbert – preached to the Seals and the Saxons in North Umbria in the 7th Century
- Sophia, Tippi, Renee, Kate, Jessica, Jennifer, Lucy, and Melissa – screen goddesses

PARTY IN THE YEAR MMIX

V. Animals

- A thirteen-striped ground squirrel, Minnesota's symbol
- Horses pulling a chariot, Bob and Nabob
- Dogs
- A cat
- A rehabilitated bald eagle, symbol of the United States of America
- Virus H1N1; missed the party

VI. Other interested persons

- Boudicca, Cleopatra, Hannibal, Spartacus, Vercingetorix, Zenobia, classy foreigners who resented Rome's ambitions,
- a very young apprentice carpenter,
- Edgar Allen Poe, who if he were alive today in his Bi-centennial year, would say, "Awfully dark in here."

VII. Questions

- Chief Hermann charged on his white horse and gained _____ (fill in blank)
- Chief Mankato charged on his white horse and gained_____ (fill in blank)
- What did the Pipebearer and the Bishops and the others discuss Saturday night?
- Name the Muse of History
- Why not take a drive to visit New Ulm?

John Hartigan Waldo

Grey Cloud Township

6-22-2009

Other books by John Hartigan Waldo:

The Kaiser's Butterfly: West of War

The Kaiser's Butterfly: West to Joy

The Kaiser's Butterfly: West to the Dragon

The Face of Qrutlx

Emm Emm Aye Aye – The Columbus Fiasco

On the Night Path (short stories)

Forthcoming:

Don't Pound Cold Iron, 2nd Edition (non-fiction)

The Spirit Island Trilogy (young readers)

www.ingramcontent.com/pod-product-compliance
Lightning Source LLC
Chambersburg PA
CBHW050922120626
46552CB00018B/2781